This book belongs to

....

....

Meet the Large family

Mr Large

Mr Large does his best to help out around the house and manages to stay calm amid the chaos created by his boisterous children.

Lester Large

Nine-year-old Lester just wants to look cool and play on his skateboard. He loves his family, but often finds them a bit embarrassing.

Luke Large

Luke is cheerful and sometimes shy. He looks up to his cool older brother Lester, but still enjoys playing with his toys, especially his old favourite, Mr Teddy.

Mrs Large

Mrs Large is always in a rush as she struggles to cope with her four children and mountains of washing. But she always has time to join in the fun!

Laura Large

Helpful and good-natured, Laura is a caring big sister to baby Lucy. She is creative and practical and enjoys making things.

Lucy Large

Lucy is the baby of the family. She gets into mischief the moment Mrs Large turns her back and her naughty little trunk finds its way into everything.

First published 2009 by Walker Books Ltd
87 Vauxhall Walk, London SE11 5HJ

2 4 6 8 10 9 7 5 3 1

Copyright © 2009 Coolabi, Go-N Productions, Luxanimation & DQ Entertainment
Based on the animation series THE LARGE FAMILY by JILL MURPHY
Developed and produced by Coolabi and Go-N Productions (France)
in association with Luxanimation and DQ Entertainment

This book has been typeset in Bembo Educational.

Printed in China

British Library Cataloguing in Publication Data: a catalogue record for this book
is available from the British Library

ISBN 978-1-4063-1986-6

www.walker.co.uk

Sebastian's Sleepover

Based on the Large Family stories by Jill Murphy

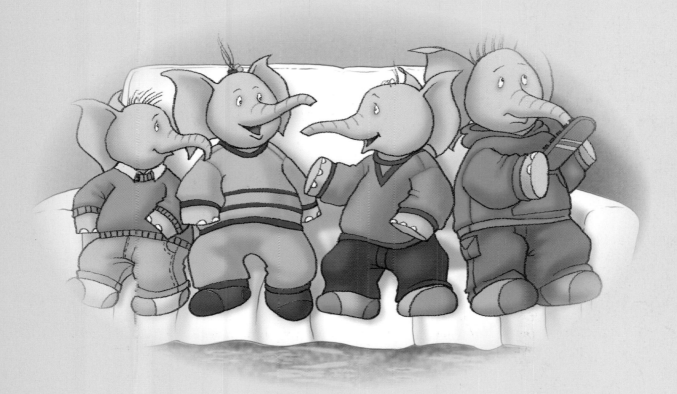

WALKER BOOKS
AND SUBSIDIARIES
LONDON · BOSTON · SYDNEY · AUCKLAND

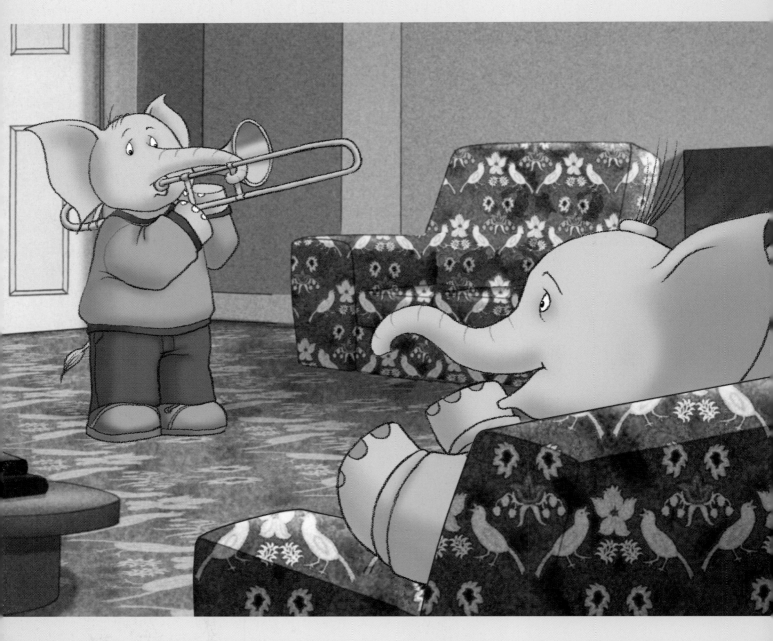

Sebastian had got top marks in his music
exam and was showing his proud mum
what he'd played.
"Bravo!" cheered Mrs Smart, as he played
the last note. "That was pure genius! As a
special treat you can choose any reward you
like. It doesn't matter how expensive it is."

"Actually," said Sebastian, "what I'd *really* like is to have Lester, Laura and Luke round for a sleepover!"

Mrs Smart looked horrified. "Are you sure?" she asked.

"Absolutely!" said Sebastian, with a big smile.

Before the children arrived, Mrs Smart covered everything in dust sheets. "Please keep your friends under control," she instructed Sebastian. "You mustn't let them play with your computer or spoil any of your things."
"Don't worry, Mum," he assured her.
"Everything will be fine."

"Have fun!" said Mrs Large, as she dropped off the excited children for their sleepover.

"Hi everyone!" welcomed Sebastian. "Come in!"
"Not yet!" instructed Mrs Smart. "Shoes off!
And don't lean on the wall, Lester. I don't want
any dirty marks."

The children sat down in a row to watch the Smarts' new television.

"Turn it down!" called Mrs Smart. "It's much too loud."

"Why don't we play a game instead?" Sebastian suggested. "How about hide and seek?"

"Good idea," said Laura. "I'll be the seeker."

Before long, Laura found everyone in
Mrs Smart's bedroom where they were
hiding in her wardrobe. She opened the
door and found everyone dressed up in
Mrs Smart's things.

Unfortunately, Mrs Smart came in and found them. "What on earth are you doing in my room?" she thundered.

"Sorry," confessed Sebastian. "It was my idea."

"Don't be silly," said Mrs Smart. "Of course it wasn't. I knew there'd be trouble if the Large children came to play. Off downstairs now, and do something quiet."

"Are you sure we're allowed to paint in the living room?" asked Laura nervously.

"Of course," replied Sebastian. "This is my special treat so we can do whatever I want. I'm so looking forward to bedtime – we can have a pillow fight."

"I don't think your mum would like that very much," said Laura.

Suddenly, Sebastian knocked the jar of green paint all over the carpet.

Mrs Smart came in and saw the mess.
"I knew it!" she yelled. "I can't trust you children for five minutes."
"It was my fault, Mum," said Sebastian. "*I* knocked it over, not them."
"Nonsense," said his mother. "Stop trying to take the blame."

Next door, Mr and Mrs Large were enjoying
the unusual peace and quiet.
"Isn't this wonderful?" said Mr Large. "We
can do anything we like!"
"How about a dance before dinner?" asked
Mrs Large.

Back at the Smarts', the children sat down
for tea.
"Pizza!" said Lester. "My favourite!"
"Look, everyone!" said Sebastian, balancing
a slice on his trunk.
"That's nothing," said Lester. "'Watch this!"
as he flipped a slice of pizza into the air and
caught it in his trunk.

"*I* can do that!" said Sebastian, throwing a slice so high in the air that it stuck to the ceiling – SPLAT! "I'll try and get it down for you," offered Lester, throwing a banana at it. The banana missed and hit Sebastian on the head.
"Right!" laughed Sebastian. "I'll get you for that." He aimed a slice of pizza at Lester.

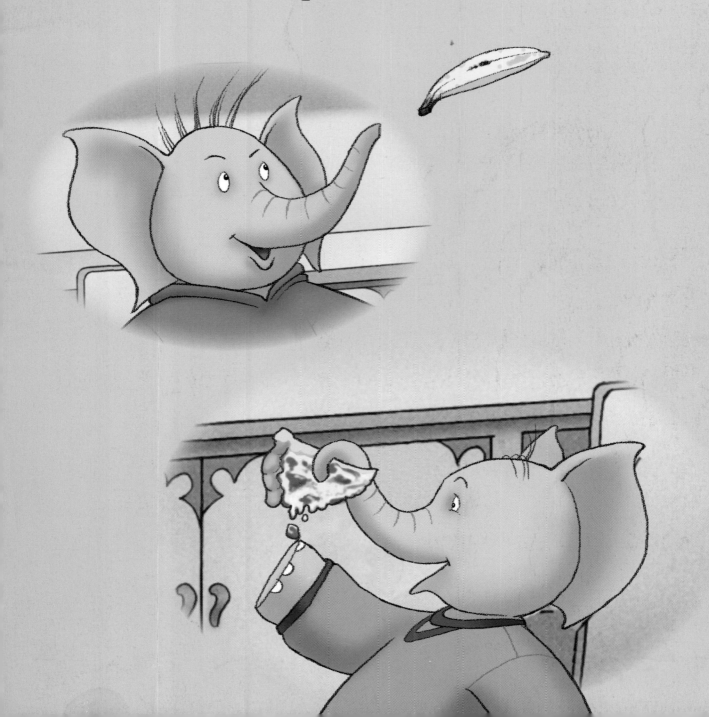

Lester ducked and the pizza hit Mrs Smart, who was coming in through the door. Everyone froze. "Who threw that?" she gasped.

"I did," said Sebastian. "I'm really sorry, Mum!"

"This is ridiculous," said Mrs Smart. "It's been bedlam since these children arrived. You can all go home – NOW!"

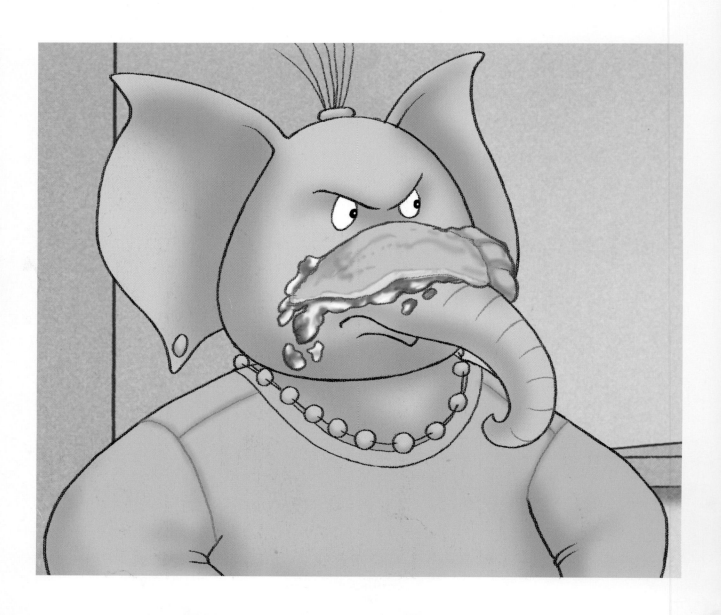

Mr and Mrs Large were dancing when the doorbell rang. They opened the door to find everyone on the doorstep. Mrs Smart was looking furious.

"Your children have wrecked Sebastian's special treat," she announced. "I knew it would be a disaster."

"Perhaps it *wasn't* a good idea," said Mrs Large.
"Could I have a different treat instead?" asked
Sebastian.
"Of course, darling!" Mrs Smart agreed.
"ANYTHING ... as long as it's not in
my house!"

"That's easy then," said Sebastian. "What I'd *really* like is to have a sleepover at the Large family house... If they'll have me, that is."
"Of course," said Mrs Large. "Perhaps we should have thought of that in the first place."

That evening, Sebastian's longed-for pillow fight was in full swing when Mrs Large came into the room.

"What's going on here?" she bellowed. Everyone froze. Then she grabbed a pillow and joined in the fun!

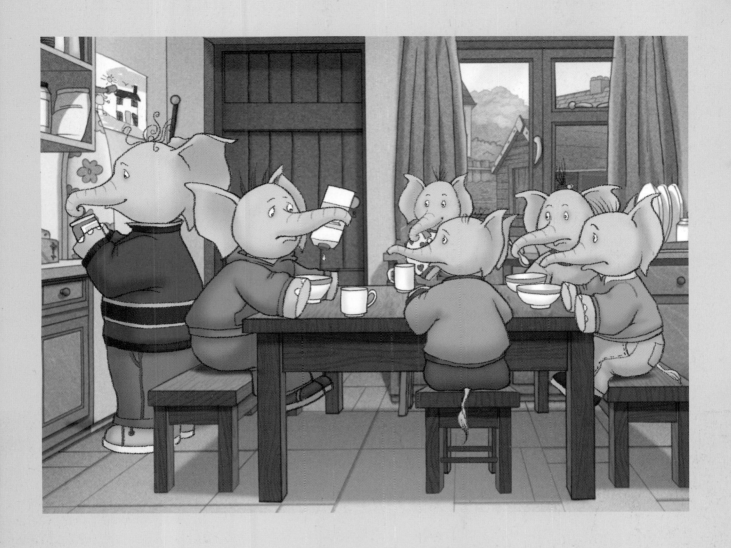

The fun was beginning to wear thin for
Sebastian next morning at breakfast when
Lester found they had run out of milk.

Next, the baby turned her bowl of cereal
upside down on her head, making a
terrible mess.

Then Mrs Large noticed smoke coming from
the toaster.
"Oh dear," she said. "The toaster's on the
blink again. Oh well, we've run out of
bread, anyway."
At this point, Sebastian decided to go home.

"That was delicious!" Sebastian announced after tucking into his breakfast back home. "Thank you, darling," said Mrs Smart proudly. "You're always guaranteed a good breakfast in this house."

"It was great fun staying next door last night," said Sebastian. "But I must admit, I'm glad to be home."

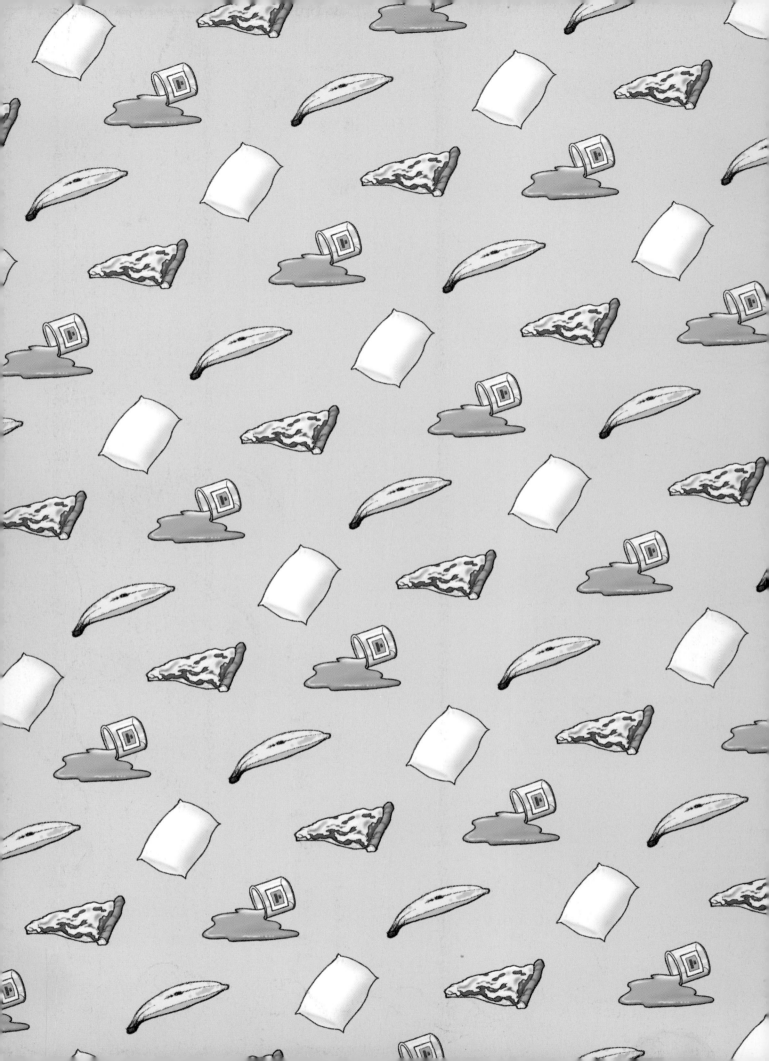

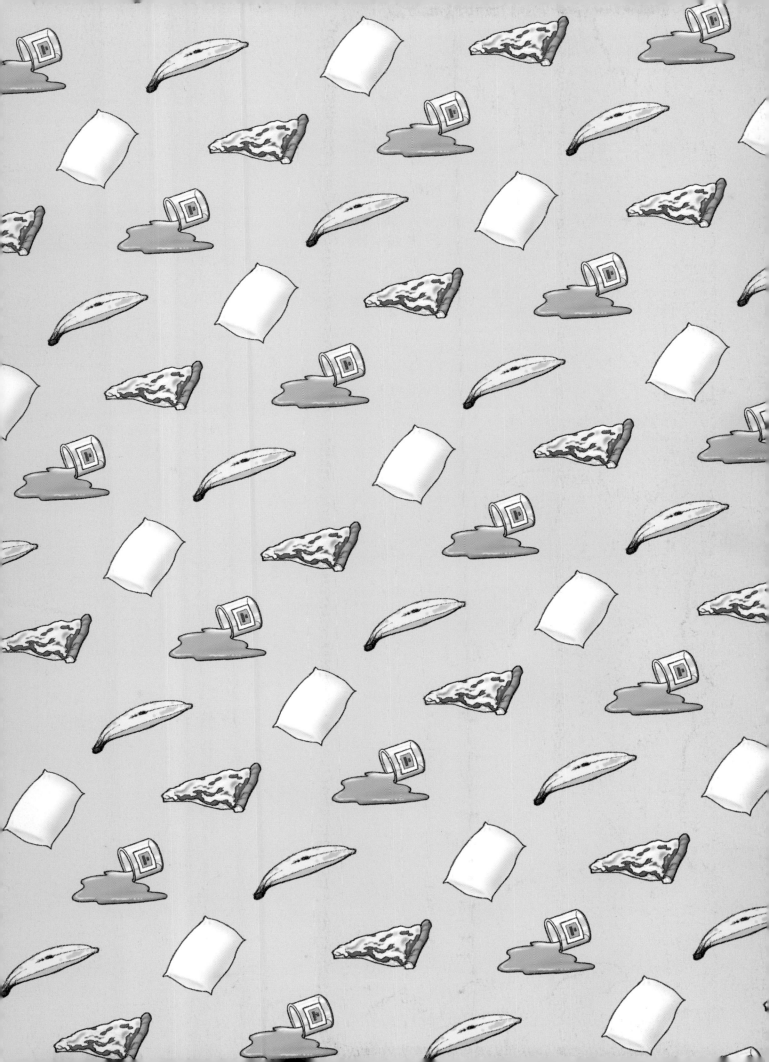

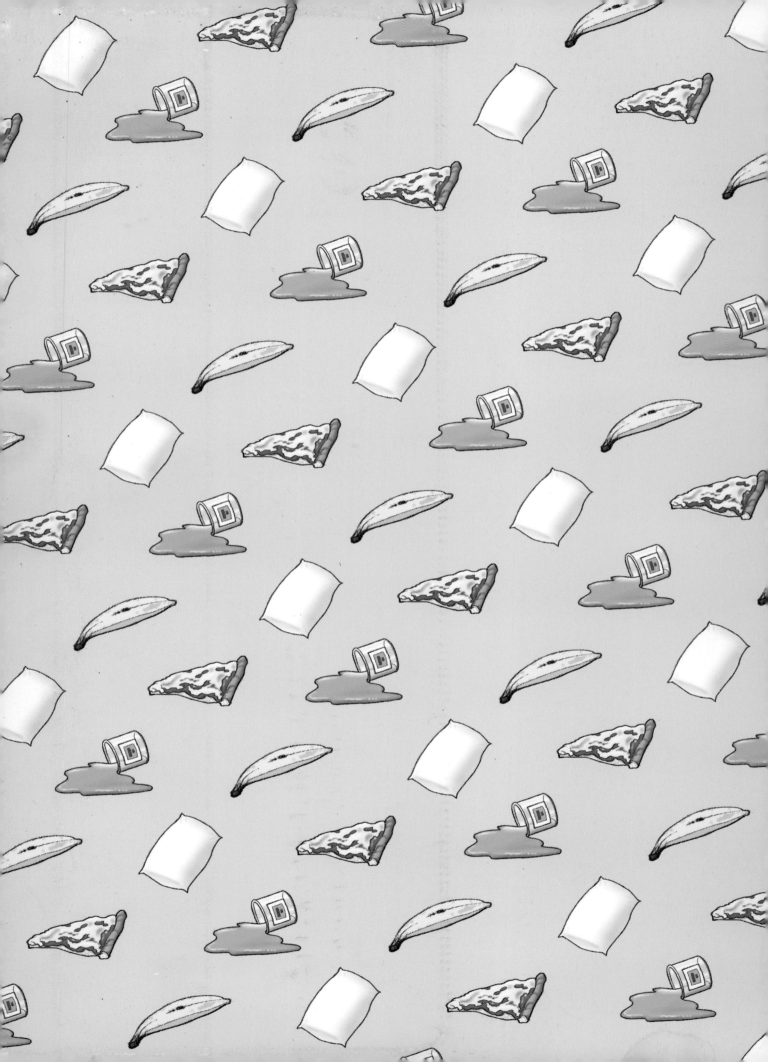